C000143115

# Two
# Miracles

MICHAEL BARRY

ISBN 979-8-88616-388-9 (paperback)
ISBN 979-8-88616-389-6 (digital)

Copyright © 2023 by Michael Barry

All rights reserved. No part of this publication may be reproduced, distributed, or transmitted in any form or by any means, including photocopying, recording, or other electronic or mechanical methods without the prior written permission of the publisher. For permission requests, solicit the publisher via the address below.

Christian Faith Publishing
832 Park Avenue
Meadville, PA 16335
www.christianfaithpublishing.com

Artwork drawn by: Anthony Palmigiano

Printed in the United States of America

I would like to dedicate this book to my wife, Dorothy, and my father, Raymond E. Barry Sr., who were very important people in Jimmy's life. During the years of Jimmy's sickness, my father would take my wife and Jimmy to all their doctors' appointments and hospital visits, while I worked during the day. He always made the time to take them to healing masses in the city, pick the kids up from school, take them to church, take them to the park, teach them sports, take them to their games, play board games, and more.

He would even take Dottie food shopping and assist with anything else she needed while I was at work. My father spent a lot of time with my family, and for that, I am forever grateful. Even as Jimmy got older, he still played sports with my father; they were very close. It was important to Jimmy that my father approved of his girlfriends, so he always introduced them to him first.

My father passed away on April 8, 1994, and I am forever grateful for the bond my family and I had with him. During this time, Dorothy and I had two more children for a total of six kids, three girls and three boys. Thanks to Dottie, my children are who they are today—wonderful adults, with families of their own.

They are all well-grounded in their faith and love their family the way their mother loved them, unconditionally. She made all occasions and holidays memorable and fun for my family. She even took on additional babysitting jobs to assist with the added expenses that came along with having a larger family, and she never complained once. She always had a beautiful, bright smile on her face that would light up a room.

After hearing me tell this story repeatedly, Dottie finally convinced me to sit down and write my story so others could share in the joy I've experienced from my encounter with *God*. I lost her after forty-nine years of love and marriage on March 20, 2016.

I didn't think much of the book till recently. In their honor, I finally decided to share my true story and spread the light of the Lord. Thanks to Christian Faith Publishing for making this book a reality for me, and a huge thank you to Dottie and my father, Raymond E. Barry Sr. to whom I miss and love very much.

# CHAPTER 1

# First Ten Years

April 27, 1973, was a great day for Dorothy and me. Our fourth child was born, Kevin John Barry. It was a really good year for us. I was working steadily. We had three other healthy children, and we were in good health. I was a brick-layer working steadily, which was a good thing back then. Steady work wasn't always easy to come by.

Around June of 1973, our older kids, Michele, Michael, and Jimmy, got sick with impetigo, a highly contagious skin disease. We couldn't travel or do much that summer because we had three sick children at home. Dorothy had to stay at home because it was a highly contagious illness, and the children needed full-time care.

Jimmy was the first to show signs of recovery and began to feel better, but sharing the same room with his sick siblings, that didn't last long. But by the end of the summer, Jimmy began to show the same symptoms of impetigo, so Dorothy continued the treatments the doctor instructed her to do. She was a mother and a nurse the entire summer of 1973.

On Wednesday, September nineteenth, I came home from work to find Jimmy laying on the couch with a slight fever. He was sick again. My wife had already contacted the doctor who said to give him some fever reducer and monitor his temperature, and she'll see improvement.

Come Thursday, he still wasn't feeling like himself. On Friday, it seemed as if he was fully recovered. He finally got to enjoy his weekend symptom-free. The following Wednesday, September twenty-sixth, my wife noticed Jimmy outside playing, but he had

an unusual limp. She called him in to see what the problem was, but by lunch, his fever spiked again.

When she called the doctor back, he had already left and began his vacation. His office sent another doctor to the house to examine Jimmy. Jimmy was given a checkup. Dottie had many questions for the doctor. "Why is his fever so high? Why did he suddenly have a limp?" The doctor claimed, "He may have fallen out of his bed and may have hit his knee." He said, "He was a boy with older siblings. It may have just been from playing rough all the time."

The doctor prescribed more medicine for his fever and told him to take it easy on his roughhousing. By Friday, Jimmy felt great again, and he was able to enjoy another good weekend. The following week, again on Wednesday, October third, I get home from work, and Jimmy is sick again. This time, he can't walk much. He's limping again, and his fever was extremely high.

We continued to give him more fever reducers and monitor his temperature throughout the day. His temperature spiked to 106! Now, that was extremely high. This time, I contacted our primary doctor. He returned from vacation. We were instructed to place Jimmy in a cold bath and if he goes into convulsions to rush him to emergency immediately, to which I said, "WHAT DO YOU MEAN if he goes into convulsions?" To which the doctor replied, "With such a high fever, it is common."

I said, "I'm bringing him to the hospital right now." I called my parents over to watch the other kids, and we rushed Jimmy right over to Jacobi Hospital. We entered a packed emergency room, but they didn't make Jimmy wait long. His fever was to the roof, still at a high of 106. They placed him in a cold bath. I'm guessing this is around 8:00 p.m. By 10:00 p.m., his fever finally returned to normal.

They examined him again, and he was scheduled to be released. The doctor said that he wanted to prescribe him more medicine for his fluctuating fever. When the doctor walks over to the admission desk, Dorothy has Jimmy on her lap, and I remember standing next to her and seeing a young doctor in a long white doctor's jacket with a stethoscope around his neck. He was a pleasant-looking man with shoulder-length brown hair.

He's walking intently toward us. When he gets closer, he says, "Hello, what a nice-looking boy you are. What's the matter with him?" To which I replied, "He has a high fever."

He then says, "He's so adorable. Do you mind if I hold him?"

I said, "Sure, if my wife is okay with that."

The young doctor then asks Dorothy if it's okay to hold Jimmy. Dorothy hands Jimmy over to the young handsome doctor. The doctor says, "Hello, Jimmy. How are you feeling today? You're such a good kid. Come; sit." The young doctor places him on the examination table. Just then, the other doctor who was off writing the prescription walks into the room.

This doctor calls him over and tells him to check Jimmy again. He shows the doctor where to place his hands on Jimmy and what to feel for. After reexamining Jimmy with the other doctor, he tells us that he's going to run more tests before releasing him. We agree, and the doctors take Jimmy to be reexamined.

Within a half-over, Jimmy returns, and they say that we have to wait on the results. Another half hour passes, and the room is filled with doctors and nurses. They took Jimmy right out of Dorothy's arms and said that he's being admitted into the hospital. Dorothy started to scream. She just didn't understand. What was going on? We were all confused.

The doctors asked me to remove Dorothy because at that point, she was out of control. Eventually, things settled down. We continued to wait on the results. The doctor returns only to tell us that Jimmy was very sick and must be admitted immediately. They told us that Jimmy needed more tests to be run, so we should go home for the evening since there was not much more we could do for him. I convince Dottie to go home.

When we get there, we find our other children asleep. We told our parents what happened with Jimmy at the hospital. Then we called Dorothy's mother and sisters to let them know as well. The next morning, I took the day off of work so Dorothy and I could go to the hospital. We get there as soon as visitation begins, and they tell us that we had to wait, so we waited.

They wouldn't let us see Jimmy. After a long while, I had to ask what was going on. I asked what was going on, but I was told that I couldn't see my son right now, but I was told that the head doctor would come meet with us soon. Until then, they couldn't do anything for us. I asked, "Look, is he really sick?" To which the nurse answers, "Yes, sir, he's very sick."

I asked, "How sick is he?"

"He's very sick, sir."

I asked, "Could he die?"

It was the first thing that blurted out. I couldn't believe they were telling me my son is not only sick but also very sick. It wasn't a question I wanted an

answer to. I really just wanted them to tell me Jimmy was going to be okay. But to my surprise, the nurse responds, "Yes, he could." I was speechless. I walked back over to Dorothy and told her, "Jimmy is 'really' sick!" We sat together in silence.

We continued to wait and wait. Finally, we see a group of young doctors approaching us. They tell us to follow them. They brought us into a private room and sat us down. All the younger interns open their notebooks and begin writing. I was determined to stay strong. There were too many people there. I just couldn't break down. No matter what they say, all I can think about is staying strong. Stay strong, Mike. Stay strong!

Dr. S—— who was in charge proceeds to explain to us that Jimmy has been diagnosed with acute lymphocytic leukemia. My wife immediately breaks down. She begins to scream and cry again. I just sat there, not knowing what to do. I felt helpless. There was nothing, as a father, I could do to help my son.

In those days, what Jimmy was diagnosed with was incurable. The survival rate for children diagnosed with ALL at that time was extremely low. Everything they could treat him with was pretty much experimental. The doctor recommended

Jimmy to continue to remain in their care because the only thing another hospital could offer us is the commonality with other parents going through the same experience with their children, but it would be a much longer commute, which would keep us away from our other children a lot more.

We decided to leave him at Jacobi Hospital and gave them permission to do whatever was necessary to heal our son. I asked to be excused. I asked Dottie to take a walk with me over to the room we had our first meeting in. We walked in and closed the door behind us, and I lost it. I just broke down. I began to cry. I threw chairs around. I punched the walls. None of it helped!

Dottie screams, "MAN up. You have to stay strong! This is going to be a long ride. Hold on tight!" I never thought she was going to be the strong one, but she straightened me right out. This gave me the strength to go in and finally see Jimmy. I walked in, only to see Jimmy had now fallen into a coma. He was just lying there. I didn't know what to do or say. It was just amazing how fast things have changed.

In an instant, our lives were turned upside down. We spent the day at the hospital learning about Jimmy's new reality, this sickness that has now taken over his beautiful child body. We learned everything we could that day—what was needed to treat him, what medicines he'll now be on, how his body will respond to the new medication.

He'll lose his hair and feel very lethargic. He'll be throwing up often. He wanted to prepare us for sleepless nights and our new reality and plenty of hospital visits. It was overwhelming. It wasn't quite registering. How have we arrived here? Why is our son sick? It was so much to take in. They asked that we go home while they continue to do tests. When we got home, we updated the family with what would now be our new reality.

Dorothy immediately went to rest, while I went up to our church, St. Francis Xavier Church in the Bronx, New York, where we were married and all our children were baptized. While kneeling and praying, I hear our parish priest come down the aisle, to which he asked, what was I doing there on a Friday afternoon? He saw me every Sunday, but he never saw me on a Friday afternoon. He knew something was going on.

I told him my son was very sick and I came to pray for him. I asked that he mention it in the weekly bulletin so my parish could pray for Jimmy. I asked that he also mention that Jimmy would need blood transfusion, and if anyone could donate blood, we would really appreciate it. He asked what hospital Jimmy was in and for more details about what was going on with him.

I told him he was being treated at Jacobi Hospital and has been diagnosed with leukemia. He couldn't believe it. He said I shouldn't expect too much from God. From what he knew about childhood leukemia, it was the killer of children, and most of the time, your prayers are unanswered. I said sarcastically, "Gee, thanks. I really needed that help."

I didn't let it affect me though because I know myself and I don't make deals with God. I couldn't promise to be a better or worse person because of the results of my prayers, so I continued to say, "Our Father," emphasizing on "His will be done." I couldn't stop saying it. I said it over and over again. I knew whatever God decided, I would have no choice but to accept it anyway.

I just prayed he wouldn't take my son. I prayed that my son be healed, not taken from me, but if that was *his* will, I would have no choice but to accept it. I would never turn my back on God. That Sunday, our parish priest did as I asked and mentioned it at every mass and placed it in the weekly bulletin. I continued to pray, especially to the Blessed Virgin Mary. I prayed to her because I knew it would be hard for a son not to answer his mother. So I continued to pray to her.

I prayed for my son's life and that he wouldn't be taken from me. All I could think of is if my son died, how in the world would I be the strong Irish man I'm known to be? I knew I was a sinner, but I didn't want my son to pay for my sins. I couldn't handle such a heartbreak. I just kept asking the Blessed Mother to spare Jimmy's life. He has so much more to live for. This could not be the end of his journey. He had so much more to offer this world. But I knew whatever God decided, I would have no choice but to accept his will.

The next day, we returned to the hospital, and Jimmy was still in a coma. It was the day my friend, Richie, was marrying Carol. We spent the day at the hospital just staring at Jimmy and praying. That night, we decided to attend the reception for Richie and Carol. Everyone wanted to know more. It was a lot. We didn't stay long. It was impossible to enjoy ourselves.

We returned to the hospital to say, "Good night, Jimmy," then returned home to our other children. The following week, many people came forward to donate blood. There was a dance at St. Francis Xavier School. My friend, Danny, gave a speech about my son and my family. It was fantastic. I think everyone in attendance donated blood that day.

Mike, the bricklayer shop steward, happened to mention it on his job site and asked his workers to donate. They even showed up. I had over eighty-five donors for the first week. It was very humbling. Even the blood bank said that they've never seen so many volunteers donate their blood. Again, I was humbled.

It was a very tough week, but we had the support of our family and neighbors. Dorothy and I gained strength from all this support, and we stuck together like glue, but Jimmy's health wasn't improving. He was still in a coma, which now was all week, and it just didn't look good.

When we returned to the hospital, we were assigned a new doctor. A young guy, he was really a good doctor once we got to know him. We loved him almost immediately. He was honest with us from the start. He said that by the end of the week, we'll know Jimmy's destiny. He'll either heal and pull through or die.

After the initial shock, he explained the treatments involved, which included a transfusion in which he needed eight donors for, to which I reply, "Where do you want me to get eight donors from?" To which he says, "You don't have eight friends?"

I said, "Check my records. I've had eighty-five donors already."

He said, "I didn't realize that, but I'll need an additional eight donors. I've never donated blood before, but I'll be the first to donate for Jimmy, so now, all you need is seven donors."

I begin to contemplate where I will find additional donors. At this point, my friend, Richie, came home from his honeymoon, and I explained to him all that was going on. I ask him, "Where am I going to find an additional seven donors?" He marched right up to the store where he worked and explained to his boss, Carmine, what was going on. Carmine then recruited his entire staff to donate the next day before work began.

I now had my seven fresh, new donors of blood thanks to more people who cared. That Monday, Jimmy was scheduled to have his transfusion. I couldn't bear to sit there and wait all day for the outcomes. I just didn't have the courage to stay. I told Dorothy that I had to go to work. She understood, and I went to work.

Before Jimmy's transfusion, the family gathered at the hospital, and we prayed over Jimmy. Before my brother, Tommy, left, he told me to light a St. Jude candle.

I told him I didn't go through saints. I go straight to the top source, the Blessed Mother.

My brother hands me a dollar and tells me, "Please, Mike, pick up a St. Jude candle, and pray to him."

The next morning, I was on my way to work downtown, by the World Trade Center. I got down there early. On my way, I passed a Catholic church, and I went in. I get to the back, and there is a statue of St. Jude standing right next to the Blessed Mother. I walked over and lit a candle to St. Jude and said, "Hey, St. Jude, that's from my brother, Tom. He'll talk to you about it."

I then turn to the Blessed Mother. After praying to the Blessed Mother for a while, I said, "Why not go to mass?" I went to mass, not realizing it was one of those churches that dedicate their daily masses to saints, St. George's Chapel. I'll never forget it. The mass I happened to attend was dedicated to St. Jude. What are the chances?? I couldn't believe it!

They had the prayer to St. Jude printed out and laid on the pews. I've never read the St. Jude prayer in all the years I've been going to church. This time was different. I read it and realized why my brother wanted me to pray to St. Jude. The prayer is about when everyone else gives up hope and it seems impossible that anything will work out, you pray to St. Jude, and he'll fix it.

I said to myself, "Holy cow, you have to be kidding me!" So I began to pray to St. Jude at this point. I asked for his help. The great thing about St. Jude is the deal you make with him is to just share the good news of St. Jude. Tell everyone he helped you out when he does. I made a deal with St. Jude. "I will tell everyone who will listen that you helped." I continued to pray and pray.

Then I returned to pray to the Blessed Mother. I then returned to work. While working all morning, I couldn't stop thinking what a real piece of garbage I was. I was at work and not at the hospital with my wife, being there for her. What a real chicken I am to run out and go to work instead of being there for her and my sick child. But it's just the way I'm built.

Now, it's lunch time, and here I am at the bar going to get drunk. It's what I did. I couldn't face it. I called my friend, Greg, and told him I'll be up to visit, but I don't want to talk about Jimmy. I just want beer and booze because getting drunk was the goal, and that's exactly what we did. Dorothy and I got drunk, and on our way home, we stopped for another drink at the local bar.

When we were headed home, I backed up my car and smashed right into a truck. I just pulled off and headed home. I woke up on my front stairs with my daughter's pillow under my head. She said that I looked uncomfortable. Jimmy was still in a coma, so that didn't help, but it was my escape that night. It was how I began to cope with my new reality.

Now, Jimmy is scheduled to get his transfusion, and I'm at a bar yet again. I ordered a beer and a shot. The shot and beer come, and all of a sudden, this feeling comes over me that tells me to call the hospital. I called the hospital, and they said, "Mr. Barry, I'm so glad you called. It's a miracle! Jimmy's fever broke during the transfusion."

I said, "How is that a miracle?

They said, "Never has a patient's fever reduced during the procedure."

I went back to the bar and gave the bartender back his drinks, and I went straight to the church. I prayed to St. Jude and couldn't stop thanking him. I couldn't believe the impossible became possible. I began to tell everyone about St. Jude. I told everyone the story, anyone who was willing to listen.

# CHAPTER 2

# The Next Ten Years

I told everyone who would listen to the story. I even told those who wouldn't listen. While at the chiropractor's office, I begin to tell him the story. Now, the chiropractor was referred to me by my brother-in-law who is an atheist, which to this day I still pray for. So here I am thinking he's probably an atheist too.

He starts asking me all types of questions. I told him that one day, I was sitting up with my son after he awoke from the coma, which was the week after his transfusion. My wife and I were with Jimmy every day and night. My daughter's, Michele's, birthday was coming up, and all she prayed for was for her brother, Jimmy, to be home for her birthday.

Between working and back and forth to the hospital, it took a toll on our entire family. There was truly a village helping us get through this time. One evening, I was sitting alone with Jimmy after my wife had gone home from the hospital. Jimmy had fallen asleep, and all I could think of was how lucky I was that this random doctor came to tell our primary doctor where to look to find Jimmy's disease.

I was so grateful that he asked him to run more tests. All I could think was how grateful I was for this man's decision. If it wasn't for him, Dottie and I would have taken Jimmy home, and he would have died. With Jimmy asleep, all I could think of was, *Let me go find this doctor who helped my son so much.* If it wasn't for him, who knows what would have happened.

I get to the emergency room, and I spot our primary doctor who admitted Jimmy. He asked how Jimmy was, and I told him, "So much better. He's no longer in a coma, and he seems to be responding to the medication." I say, "Hey, Doc, I would like to talk with you about the doctor on call the night Jimmy was diagnosed."

He says, "Who? HIM?" And he points to the doctor next to him.

I said, "No, not him, he was a young handsome guy with long brown hair."

"No, no," the doctor says, "this guy right here was the only one on call with me that night."

I said, "No, there was another young fella who came to hold Jimmy that evening while you stepped away. He showed you where to feel and touch to find what was going on with Jimmy that night."

The doctor says, "What are you talking about?"

I said, "Doc, how could you not remember? You told me I could take Jimmy home, and this doctor asked you to run more tests before releasing him."

The doctor says, "Mr. Barry, I think you're mistaken. I was never asked by another doctor to run tests. I decided to run them myself before releasing him."

I said, "Doc, you have got to be kidding me?"

I just walked away. I couldn't believe this guy thinks I'm making this shit up. He's trying to take credit for giving Jimmy more tests, but I know for sure this younger fella was the one who asked him to do it. I went over to talk to the nurse who was also asking for Jimmy and how he was doing. So I asked her about the doctors on call that evening, and she too tells me there were no other doctors on call that evening that met that description.

At this point, I'm angry. These people think I'm lying about another doctor being on call. What would I gain from that? I say, "Why won't you admit there was another doctor on call the evening Jimmy was diagnosed?" To which she replies, "Mr. Barry, there were only two doctors on call that evening." I say, "Fine. Somehow, I would get to the bottom of this."

This is extremely important to my family. The next day, I told Dorothy I went down to find the nice young fella who helped Jimmy that evening, and she asked if I talked with him. I told her they wouldn't even tell me who he was. I guess they wanted to take credit for running more tests on Jimmy and not releasing him that evening.

But I'm determined to find this guy. I must thank him myself. Then Dr. Louie says, which shocked me all together, especially since I thought he was an atheist, "You know what, Mike? You had two miracles happen to you, not one," to which I replied, "What do you mean two miracles?"

He said, "You had the miracle of St. Jude in getting his fever to break, and the other one was either God himself or an angel he sent to show your doctor where to feel for Jimmy's issues."

I said, "What are you talking about?"

He said, "Doctors don't get medals for admitting kids into the hospital. The doctor probably never saw the guy you're talking about. It was either an angel or God himself who placed his hands on Jimmy when he asked to hold him."

I said, "You've got to be kidding me?"

He said, "No, I'm serious… It was either an angel or God himself."

I said, "Wow, I never thought of that."

For the next ten years, I tell the story of having two miracles happen and how God or an angel came down to find Jimmy's illness and sent St. Jude to take care of his fever. In the meantime, we had two more children—Jamie, born on October 17, 1975, and another baby girl, Maryann, born on July 1, 1984. This is the way I'm telling the story of my two miracles.

# CHAPTER 3

# The Next Ten Years

It's 1999, and I'm in church with my youngest daughter, Maryann. We attended morning mass that day. I've raised my kids to go to church every Sunday. Never have I pushed religion down their throats, but I pray they live as good Catholics and pass it on to the future generations. Maryann is now fifteen years old. During mass, they announce they're going to have a special prayer request for Sister Faustina Kowalska to become a saint. They're going to have a prayer meeting at 3:00 p.m. this afternoon.

This Sister Faustina has seen God. She once requested a picture be painted of him. She had to seek an artist to bring her vision of God to life, exactly the way he looked. So my daughter asks, "Daddy, do you want to come back at 3:00 p.m. today?" Here I am thinking, *Wow, a fifteen-year-old wanting to go back to church*, so I said, "Absolutely!"

At 3:00 p.m., we walked back up to church to see what the mass was all about. As we enter the church, they give us a prayer book, which tells us that there's a new way to say the rosary. They have a big picture of God on the altar. We are all praying to the pope at this point to make this woman a saint. It was her third proven miracle, and she was up for sainthood. We stayed for the entire mass. I took the booklet home with me.

The next day, it was freezing. I was working out in Brooklyn. I was on a job with my three sons and son-in-law. I'm the bricklayer foreman on this site. I couldn't really put anyone to work but the laborers, setting up the job site. I couldn't leave because I had to oversee the work being done. I went to the shanty, looked over the plans, and made some calls. I finished up early, so I decided to take the prayer book out and try the new version of the rosary.

I began to say the rosary while staring at the picture of God. While looking at the picture, I realize that if you put a white doctor's jacket on this man in the picture and hang a stethoscope around his neck, it was like getting hit with a sledgehammer. This is the young man who came down the hallway in the hospital the evening Jimmy was diagnosed and asked to hold Jimmy.

It hit me. This is the man who held my child that night. I was flabbergasted. I couldn't believe this. I didn't know what to do. All I could think of was to tell everyone who was willing to listen to the story and to write this book and keep my promise to St. Jude. I came home that evening and showed Dorothy the picture. I put my hand over his body to just reveal the face, and I asked her if she would put a white doctor's jacket on him, who is this guy? She knew immediately. That's the doctor that asked to hold Jimmy that evening.

"We finally found him," she said. At this point, we both realized there is no doubt in our minds that we met Jesus the evening Jimmy was diagnosed. It was his decision to let our son live. I continue to thank him daily for all my blessings. I still stop over at his statue at the end of each mass on Sunday, hold his feet, and thank *him* for walking down the hallway that day in the hospital and saving my son's life.

After Jimmy came out of coma, my daughter's birthday was the thirtieth, and she prayed every night for her brother to come home from the hospital. On October 29 after work, I went to see Jimmy in the hospital. It was pouring out, very dark, and dreary, so I stopped by our home to see my kids, only to realize Dorothy was still at the hospital. I headed straight to the hospital.

When I got off the elevator, I was soaked. I saw Dorothy standing there with Jimmy in her arms, saying, "Hurry up. Hurry up. Go back home, and get his clothes. We are taking him home."

I said, "Are you nuts? We can't take him home tonight. Have you seen the weather out there?"

She said, "They are releasing Jimmy tonight, Mike. We are taking him home. Get on the elevator, go back to the house, and get his clothes NOW! He is coming home with us tonight!"

I didn't hesitate to do as she says. I went right back home, got his clothes, and headed right back to the hospital. We got him dressed and signed him out. We took him home. He was home the evening of October 29, right on time for his sister's birthday, which answered her prayers.

For three years, it was very difficult. He slept with us every night. He would throw up every night. It wasn't easy for him. He was on all types of medications including chemo and radiation, which caused him to lose his hair. Again, thank God for my parents, friends, and neighbors. They helped us so much.

My father would drive Dorothy everywhere while I was at work. He would take Jimmy for treatments and helped in so many ways, all the while Dorothy is pregnant with our daughter, Jamie, who was born October 17, 1975. Jamie was a sick child as well. She had asthma attacks that always led to pneumonia, which led her to spend a period of time in the hospital as well.

We had a rough journey but always made the best of it. Jimmy's birthday was on St. Patrick's Day, so we always made sure we celebrated his life. We had tons of people over, and we got really drunk. It always ended the same way, with Dorothy in front of Jimmy's bedroom just crying and saying, "We have to tell him that he'll never be able to have children," which was one of the things the doctor told us would be the result of all the medications he was taking.

Every St. Patrick's Day, we would go through the same thing. We would have a great day. Then that evening, we would have to discuss when and how we would tell Jimmy. I told her, "It wasn't the time, and we should wait till he's older and tell him when he's engaged, when he wants to start a family." There was no use worrying about him at such a young age. It wasn't something a kid his age should be thinking about.

After numerous arguments with Dorothy about when we would tell Jimmy he would never have children, she finally agreed, and we waited. The crying continued year after year, after every party. During this time, Jimmy got bigger, healthier, and stronger. He attended St. Francis Xavier Grammar School where he learned to play sports with his classmates. He played basketball, baseball, and bowling.

During the summers, he learned to swim and practiced martial arts with his brothers. Whenever I could, I would take him and his brothers to work with me on a construction site. They loved it. They loved going to work with me. The harder I put them to work, the more I enjoyed it. They never complained about anything.

When Jimmy wasn't playing with brothers or friends, he was down the block at his grandparents' house. He loved them. He always wanted to hang out with them. My father and Dottie continued monitoring his health and taking him to all his appointments. At that point, he was off all medications, and his hair grew back beautifully.

After Jimmy graduated from grammar school, he went on to attend Mount St. Michael HS, where he became an *all-star* football player and a good student. During the summer, he would work in construction with his older brother and me. Throughout his childhood, he always talked about being a police officer. He finally got a chance to take the police test and passed with flying colors and was accepted into the police academy.

After graduation, he was assigned to the forty-third precinct, a rough precinct in the Bronx, New York. After receiving several awards for his police work, he was then promoted to detective and assigned to Bronx narcotics where he served the remainder of his time as a police officer.

Jimmy got engaged on September 24, 1995. Now, we have to tell him. We have to tell him and his future wife. We called a meeting with him and told his future wife, Mary, all about how sick Jimmy was as a child, all the medications he was on, and how the doctors told us he may never have children. The entire time we were telling her the story, you could tell Mary was getting very upset over the news. Jimmy didn't have much of a response.

After the discussion, we asked Mary if she had any other questions. She asked for the doctor's information. She wanted to speak with him herself. We gave her the information. I looked over at Jimmy to ask if he's okay. He said he was all right. I asked if he was sure and what he thought about all that we have shared with him. His response was exactly what I wanted to hear. It was a proud moment for me.

I knew I did my job when he said, "Dad, if God wants me to have children, I will. He has the final say. I'll be okay." Jimmy and Mary got married a few months later. They showed up to our house and announced they're having a child. Jimmy and Mary have two healthy sons. The doctor could never tell us Jimmy was cured, but we knew we had God on our side.

Jim, Mary, Big Jim and Sean

Jimmy his mother and two sons

I thank him daily for walking down that aisle in the hospital that evening and saving our son. I thank my wife, Dorothy, for always being there for me and for my six children, for raising them to be the people they're today. I would like to thank Jacobi Hospital for everything they did for our child, Jimmy. We are forever grateful to them. I would like to thank Dr. —— for helping us make the decision to stay at Jacobi Hospital.

I would like to thank my brother, Tom, for telling me about St. Jude. I would like to thank my entire village, Pat and Ray, Anne and Tom, Peggy and Johnnie, Dot and Hughie, Betty and Bob, Elenore and Kevin, Irene and Greg, and the whole Penny family. They were always there when we needed them.

I thank my neighbors, Rose and Bob, Lucy and John, Lyla and Morris, Fran and Jerry, Carol and Richie, and Sandra and Barry. This neighborhood came together during such a difficult time, and I can't say enough to all of them who were all so great to us and also for Father Joe Rossitto and Father Ralph Verdi, who always prayed for our family.

I want to thank St. Jude. He really made the impossible possible. I thank the Blessed Mother Mary. I want to thank Dr. Louie for letting me know that I experienced two miracles and to never lose sight of all the miracles that surround us. I want to thank my daughter, Maryann, for asking me to attend the mass for Sister Faustina. I want to thank the pope for making Sister Faustina a Saint.

I want to thank a bricklayer named Earl for making me sit down to write this book so everyone knows that there are miracles still occurring today. I also want to thank Bill Maher for being such an atheist. I listened to him on the Maher show on August 20, 2005, which encouraged me to share this story with you all.

I don't want anyone to listen to his sick views on God. There is a God, and he is very present today. Like always, I thank the Blessed Mother, St. Jude, and God himself for being there for me. Thanks to all my children for sticking together and remaining good Catholics.

Michael his wife and two grandsons

Another part of this story is my brother, Tom, who was a bricklayer foreman for one of the top bricklayer companies in New York City. He worked for a big company called La Salle, who used to do all the high-rises in downtown Manhattan and department buildings.

Three years after Jimmy got sick, things were getting tight, and La Salle started branching off into other work. At this point, Jimmy was five years old, and La Salle was bidding a job, and it happened to be at St. Jude Church in Fordham section of the Bronx, and they picked my brother, Tom, to be the bricklayer foreman for this job.

Tom took this assignment with great enthusiasm and pride to do this church for St. Jude. It really meant something to him. They started laying it out and did all the block work first, and when the time came to lay the first brick, he brought my son, Jimmy, who was five years old at the time, to lay the first brick in St. Jude Church.

It was a great honor from my brother, Tom, and my son, Jim, to be a part of this construction project. Today, Jimmy is a retired police officer and has two beautiful sons and a lovely wife. It's August of 2005, and I finally got this story on tape. I hope someone reads this book and gets to know *God*.

# ABOUT THE AUTHOR

I was born in the Bronx, New York, in 1945, and my wife, Dorothy, was born Dorothy J. Clarke in the Bronx, New York, in 1946. We both lived on the same block growing up, and it's where our journey began. I attended St. Francis Xavier Grammar School, and she went to the public school in the neighborhood.

We spent our summer days on Orchard Beach or the local Bronx pool with our friends. We both attended Columbus HS. At the age of fifteen, in 1960, I asked her to go steady, and she agreed. We have been together ever since.

After graduation, I became a bricklayer, and she went to work in Manhattan as a secretary in the bank. We got married in 1967 and had our first of six children in 1968. Before we married, Dorothy, who was raised Protestant, converted to Catholicism, and we raised our children in the Catholic Church.

Dorothy lost her father when she was pregnant with our first daughter, Michele Barry, in the late sixties, and we bought her parents' house in the Bronx, New York, where we raised our family and where I still reside today.

Ingram Content Group UK Ltd.
Milton Keynes UK
UKHW021145120323
418423UK00011B/210

9 798886 163889